DATE DUE

J

The Type One
Super Robot

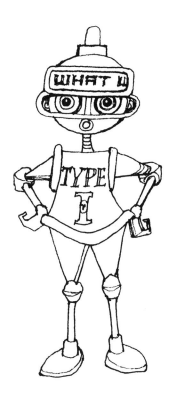

The Type One Super Robot

ALISON PRINCE
with illustrations by the author

FOUR WINDS PRESS
New York

This book is for Marilyn Malin, who suggested the idea.
With love, and thanks for many years of help and friendship.

Four Winds Press
Macmillan Publishing Company
866 Third Avenue, New York, NY 10022
Printed in the United States of America
First published 1986 in Great Britain by Marilyn Malin Books in association
with Andre Deutsch, London
First American edition 1988

10 9 8 7 6 5 4 3 2 1

The text of this book is set in 12 point Sabon.

Library of Congress Cataloging-in-Publication Data
Prince, Alison.
The Type One Super Robot.
Summary: While spending the summer together, a boy and
his uncle acquire a household robot with a mind of its own.
[1. Robots—Fiction. 2. Uncles—Fiction.
3. Humorous stories] I. Title.
PZ7.P9358T4 1988   [Fic]   87-14835
ISBN 0–02–775201–1

81200

Contents

Manders Arrives   1

Manders Flies   27

Manders Solves a Problem   49

Manders Goes Shopping   67

Manders Comes Home   91

Manders Arrives

One morning, Humbert's mother opened a letter at breakfast and read it with growing excitement. "They want me to go on a lecture tour!" she said. "All over the country, talking to people about arranging dried grass. I'll be away the whole summer. Isn't it wonderful, Arthur!"

"Yes, very wonderful," said Humbert's father. "But what about Humbert?"

"He could come," said Millicent.

"No, thank you," said Humbert politely. "I don't think I would be interested in dried grass. Not to last all through the summer."

"I shall be busy," said Arthur.

"We know," said Millicent and Humbert together. Arthur went to The City every day with a briefcase and a neatly rolled umbrella, and he did not do practical things like looking after Humbert.

Arthur stirred his tea and said, "There are various aunts."

"Yes," said Millicent thoughtfully. "Three close-by."

"Will I like them?" Humbert asked nervously.

"I don't know," said his mother. "We'll have to try them out and see."

So, after several telephone calls, Humbert and his mother set out on a tour of aunt sampling.

The first aunt was Cornelia, who had seven children of her own. They seemed, Humbert thought, rather wild.

"Humbert?" said Cornelia. "Oh, I'll never notice he's here, not with all this lot. As long as he does his part."

Humbert removed himself from his undignified position in a puddle underneath several of the children and said politely that he could not be sure he would enjoy doing his part.

"You'll love it," said Cornelia. She set a huge basin of semolina pudding on the table with seven spoons and gave Humbert an eighth. "There you are," she said. "Dig in. Since you're a visitor, I'll give you a start before the gang gets at it."

"I think I'd rather not," said Humbert.

So he and his mother went home.

3

The next aunt was Edie, who, together with Uncle Willis, kept a huge garden beautifully tidy.

"Humbert," said Edie vaguely as she did something with raffia, "ah, yes. Mind those flower pots, dear. The whole summer. I expect that'll be all right. As long as he helps with thinning the plants."

"And potting them," said Uncle Willis.

Humbert was already beginning to wilt in the hot greenhouse. He had collided with a cactus, and something with tendrils was tickling his neck. He looked at the trays and trays of seedlings and the hundreds and hundreds of little pots that they had to go into, and said politely that he didn't think he had green fingers.

Edie and Willis were battling with a collapsed passionflower and seemed to have forgotten about Humbert.

He and his mother went home.

Then there was an aunt called Dot, who lived in a house absolutely crammed with dead butterflies in little boxes. There were stuffed birds, too, and brass trays and glass knickknacks and teapots shaped like cottages. In the middle of it all, Dot sat in a huge, dumpy armchair and knitted something with a lot of balls of wool which were in a terrible tangle.

"Humbug?" said Dot.

"No, *Humbert*," said Millicent loudly. "To stay with you."

"Yes, Humbug can stay if he likes," said Dot. "I'll teach him to knit. We'll be ever so cozy. He can help me untangle my wool, if he's good. As long as he doesn't mind dusting."

There was an awful lot of dust, Humbert thought. He glanced around and met the angry eye of a stuffed sea eagle. He backed away from it nervously and bumped into a folding table whose top was a brass tray stacked with wax flowers, mirrors, and a lighthouse made of shells. The table folded itself up, and all the things fell

on the floor, and there was a lot of confusion, after which Dot said she didn't think Humbug was at the cozy age yet.

So Humbert and his mother went home.

"Oh, dear," sighed Millicent. "What *are* we to do? Time is getting short, and the other aunts are far-flung, living up Italian mountains or in Hong Kong flats. Sampling them will be expensive and time-consuming, and my first lecture on arranging dried grass is due next week."

"There's always Bellamy," said Arthur.

There was a long pause. Millicent and Arthur looked at each other doubtfully, then Humbert asked, "Is Bellamy another aunt?"

"Bellamy is an uncle," said Millicent. "He is my brother. But, to be frank, I am not sure if he is capable of looking after you."

"Why not?" asked Humbert.

There was another pause, then Millicent said, "What he needs is help. But people won't stay."

"Can't blame them," said Arthur. He frowned thoughtfully, then said, "I wonder if he'd take to a robot? That might be the answer."

"Brilliant!" said Millicent.

"What sort of robot?" asked Humbert.

"Mechanized help," said his father. "A machine that does everything. I know a chap in The City who runs a robot manufacturing business. If we're going to see Bellamy, I'll bring him along."

"Do that," said Millicent.

Next day, Humbert and his mother set out to see Uncle Bellamy, together with Arthur and his friend Trev from The City.

Uncle Bellamy lived in a small, plain house in the middle of a lot of nettles.

"You see what I mean," said Arthur as they fought their way up the path.

"Needs a robot," agreed Trev.

The front door stood open, and the sound of a typewriter came from somewhere upstairs.

"Bellamy!" called Millicent. "We're here!"

"Be down in a minute," came a distant voice. "Find somewhere to sit."

"Easier said than done," muttered Arthur.

Humbert saw what he meant. The chairs and the rather battered sofa were covered with books and newspapers and the remains of several snack lunches, which looked as if they had mostly consisted of sardine sandwiches. In the middle of the most comfortable armchair lay a large tabby cat surrounded by empty sardine tins. Its whiskers looked slightly oily and it was purring loudly, with its eyes shut.

Arthur, Trev, and Millicent perched on the arms of chairs and Humbert squeezed himself into the chair beside the cat. Several sardine tins fell on the floor as he did so.

Footsteps came clattering down the carpetless stairs, and Uncle Bellamy came into the room. He looked wispy, Humbert thought, and a hole in the sleeve of his sweater was mended with a safety pin.

Millicent sighed when she saw her brother. "After all these years, Bellie, you haven't changed," she said.

"Millicent, please do not call me Bellie," said Uncle Bellamy. "After all these years, I thought you might have stopped doing that."

"As eccentric as ever." Millicent sighed.

Uncle Bellamy saw Humbert sitting beside the cat and smiled. "You found Goblin," he said. "Nice cat really, so long as he's fed. People are the same, on the whole. Are you going to come and stay here?"

"Yes, please," said Humbert, who had already made up his mind. Then he added, "As long as I what?"

Uncle Bellamy looked inquiring. "Don't get you," he said.

"The various aunts," Humbert explained, "all said I could stay if I liked—as long as I somethinged. Did my part, or helped with the plants, or dusted."

"Oh," said Uncle Bellamy. "No, nothing like that. Do what you like, within reason."

"What's reason?" asked Humbert.

"I don't know," said Uncle Bellamy. "But I expect we'll find out, between us."

"Now, wait a minute," said Millicent. "Bell—er, Bellamy, if you really intend to look after Humbert, you'll need help."

"Help won't stay," said Uncle Bellamy simply. "It never does."

"This kind of help will," said Millicent. "It's got to. It's mechanical."

"A robot," said Arthur.

Uncle Bellamy looked alarmed. "I don't think I could manage anything like that," he said.

"Ah, but that's just the point," put in Trev. "You don't *have* to manage it. *It* manages *you.*"

Uncle Bellamy looked even more alarmed.

"We won't have any argument," said Millicent firmly. "If Humbert is coming to this house, the robot comes as well. Otherwise I shall worry about Humbert all summer. Somebody or something has to have a bit of sense in this household."

"I don't *want* a robot," said Uncle Bellamy.

"Then the deal's off," said Millicent. "Humbert will go to an aunt."

"Oh, please!" begged Humbert. "Not an aunt!"

Uncle Bellamy looked at him. "I suppose you learn all this beep-beep stuff at school, do you?" he asked. "You understand about this electronic cookery they do? All these chips and things? You could manage a robot?"

Humbert had no idea what was involved in managing

a robot, but he did not stop to think. There was a lot at stake. "Oh, yes," he said confidently. "You don't have to worry about that. I'll make sure it doesn't disturb you." Somehow, he felt as if he had known Uncle Bellamy for a long time.

"You'll be amazed at what it'll do to this place," said Trev, glancing around the untidy room. "The Type One Housemaster is a very capable machine. It came through its domestic trial with flying colors."

Uncle Bellamy closed his eyes. "I feel," he said, "that I am having a domestic trial myself."

"Yes, well, I should be getting back to The City," said Arthur, glancing at his watch. "Time is money, you know."

"Absolute rubbish," said Uncle Bellamy. "But I'd be quite glad if you'd all go, otherwise my ideas will get muddled and I'll forget what I was typing. See you Thursday, Hum."

"Right," said Humbert and smiled.

Thursday was a hot, sunny day. Humbert and his mother set out in the car for Uncle Bellamy's house, pausing on the way to collect a large, paper-wrapped box from Trev's factory in Cheam. The two white-coated men who loaded the box into the back of the car handled it with great care, and Trev gave Millicent a booklet in a plastic wrapper and said, "Instructions for the Type One Super Housemaster. You'd better tell your brother to read them carefully."

"I'll try," said Millicent. "But you know what he's like."

Trev nodded gloomily and said, "Good luck, anyway."

"You'd better give those instructions to me," said Humbert as they set off again. "I mean, I'm the one who'll be managing this robot."

"Yes," agreed Millicent. "I'm afraid you will. But it's better than nothing."

As they drove through the countryside, Humbert thought he heard music. "Is the radio on?" he asked.

"No," said Millicent. "Switch it on if you want."

"That's not what I meant," said Humbert. He stared over the back of his seat. "It's the box," he said. "It's singing."

"Oh, dear," said Millicent, slowing down a little. "I do hope Trev didn't give us the wrong one."

Humbert turned his head sideways. "It says Type One Super Housemaster on the box," he reported.

"That's all right, then," said Millicent, and drove on.

By the time they reached Uncle Bellamy's house, it was midday and very hot. The box was still singing. The front door of the house was standing open as before, and Goblin was thoughtfully licking a sardine tin on the sitting-room table. Humbert suddenly laughed.

"What's funny?" asked his mother.

"Goblin," said Humbert. "He's always gobbling."

"That's right," said Uncle Bellamy, clattering down the stairs. "That's how he got his name."

The Type One Super Housemaster stopped singing when they opened the hatch, and remained silent while it was carried into the kitchen. Humbert set about unpacking it while Millicent went back to the car to fetch Humbert's suitcase and the things she had brought for lunch.

Humbert pulled off the brown paper around the box and started prying up the stout cardboard flaps. Suddenly he realized that he was being assisted from inside the box. As he pulled, something pushed. Uncle Bellamy watched suspiciously.

"Come on," said Humbert, tugging hard, "we're nearly there."

Staples burst outward, and a broad metal hand gave a jaunty wave.

"Heaven help us," said Uncle Bellamy faintly.

Amid a shower of white packing pellets, the Type One Super Housemaster sat up and shook its head. Humbert stared at it with interest.

"What's it supposed to *do*?" asked Uncle Bellamy, scratching his beard doubtfully.

Humbert had been reading the instructions in the car, so he had the answer ready. "Anything a man does," he said.

"Man does," said Uncle Bellamy. "Manders. That would do as a name, wouldn't it? Got to call it *something*."

He had an odd way of finding names for things, Humbert thought, but it seemed to work. He looked at the robot and said experimentally, "Manders?"

A small lamp on the Type One Super Housemaster's head glowed for a moment as if in thought, then a single word marched repeatedly across the screen in the middle of its face. WHAT, it said. WHAT WHAT WHAT WHAT. . . .

"That's your name," explained Humbert.

The lamp glowed again, with a pink light this time. "Name," said the robot in a slightly husky voice. "Manders. Thank you." It climbed off the table by

18

extending telescopic legs until they touched the floor, then slid down to stand at about Humbert's height, and began to sing again.

"I hope it isn't going to do that all the time," said Uncle Bellamy.

"Sorry," said Manders, and stopped singing. His pink light faded and was replaced by a dim blue one.

"Now you've upset him," Humbert said to his uncle. "It says in the instructions that a pink light means he's happy and a blue one means he's sad."

"What about an ordinary white one?" asked Uncle Bellamy.

"Thinking," said Humbert.

Millicent came in with Humbert's suitcase and a stack of plastic food boxes. She glanced at Manders without any sign of surprise and said, "Oh, good, you're all getting to know each other. I've been talking to your neighbor, Bell, a man called Ernie. Apparently he does odd jobs for you."

"His jobs are a bit odd, yes," agreed Uncle Bellamy, who had made a face at being called Bell.

"I thought I'd better explain to him about the robot," Millicent went on, "in case he felt his job had been taken over. I was frightfully tactful, but he did seem a little put out."

Humbert looked at Manders and saw the words PUT OUT travel across his screen, followed by WHAT WHAT WHAT WHAT. "Manders is whatting again," he said. He bent down to explain. "Put out means the man was a bit cross," he said.

Manders glowed pink and said, "Thank you."

Millicent laughed and said, "You two seem to be getting on like a house on fire."

HOUSE ON FIRE flashed across the robot's screen, and with a bright blue light, Manders started up a sirenlike blare at deafening pitch and rushed across to the sink. He shot out a hand to the cold tap, turned it

20

on full and stopped blaring just long enough to shout, "Hose! Where hose!" Then he started blaring again.

"It's all right, Manders!" shouted Humbert. "The house *isn't* on fire, it's just an expression. Do stop that awful noise!"

"Oh," said Manders, his blue light fading. "Wrong. Sorry."

"Ridiculous thing," said Uncle Bellamy. "You must be out of your mind, Millicent, wishing a hysterical gadget like that on a civilized household."

"I think he's rather nice," said Humbert, taking Manders's hand protectively. "He's only trying to help."

"Help!" said Uncle Bellamy. "Any more help like that and I shall become completely unhinged."

"If you do," said Millicent, "it won't be the fault of the robot." And Humbert took his uncle's hand as well.

After a lunch of sardines provided by Uncle Bellamy and salad out of Millicent's plastic boxes, Manders washed up very efficiently, using a sponge attachment on one hand and a hot-air jet on the other. Millicent patted him on the head cautiously, causing him to beam with a grateful pink light, and said, "I really must be off. I'll see you in September, Humbert. Be good. If it stays as hot as this, you'll have a lovely summer."

"And I shall melt," said Uncle Bellamy. "It's absolutely frying in my room. You'll find a little puddle under the typewriter which used to be me."

"Nonsense," said Millicent. "Get the robot to do something about air conditioning. It probably can."

Manders began whatting again and Humbert said, "I'll explain later."

Uncle Bellamy said, "Madness," and stumped off upstairs.

When Humbert had waved good-bye to his mother, he turned to Manders, who was waving as well, and said, "Right. Now we can get on with our summer. Can you fly a kite?"

Manders thought. Then, as Humbert had rather expected, his screen began a parade of WHATs.

"Kite," said Humbert. "Big flat thing with a long string on it. Flying. You know—moving about in the air."

"Thank you," said Manders. "I will try. Where is kite?"

"We haven't made it yet," said Humbert. "But there's

all that brown paper your box was wrapped in, and yards of string it was tied up with, and we could use those thin metal bits out of its edges to make the kite's cross pieces."

PAPER, STRING, AND METAL BITS flitted across Manders's screen, and then he said, "Yes. Shall I make it?"

"If you think you can," said Humbert. "That would be great. And while you're making the kite, I'll go and have a look around for a good place to fly it. The garden won't do, because it's full of nettles, but there seems to be a hill behind it. I'll be back soon."

"Yes," said Manders, and returned to the kitchen in brightly lit-up thought.

Humbert went along the path that ran beside the garden. It led through a midgy kind of wood where the trees were so close together that the sunshine came through only in speckles, but it led out onto the steep, grassy hill Humbert had seen from the kitchen window. He climbed right up to the top and there, a little breathless, stared down at the houses, which looked as small as a toy village below him. He saw that the road running past Uncle Bellamy's house came to a bridge over a stream, and decided to go and have a look at it. There might be tadpoles in it, or sticklebacks—good for a dull day when there was no wind for kite flying.

He made his way back down the hill and found the stream, though it was much farther than it had looked from the hilltop. He dabbled about with a twig boat for a bit, then went back to the house to see if Manders had finished the kite.

23

Inside the kitchen was an amazing creation.

"Kite," said Manders proudly.

Humbert stared at it. "No," he said. "I don't know what it is, but it isn't a kite."

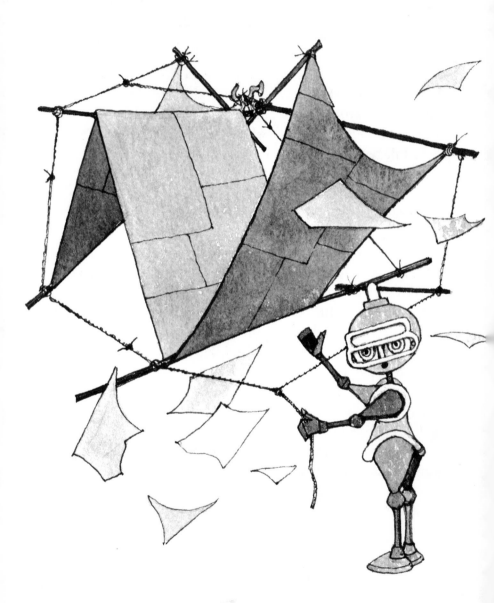

"Move about in the air," protested Manders. "Fly." He pulled the string to show what he meant, and the contraption moved to and fro. It made quite a strong wind, and sent the remaining scraps of brown paper flapping around the kitchen.

"Flying means going right up into the sky," Humbert explained. "Out-of-doors. No, don't go blue, Manders. It isn't your fault. I thought you understood."

The words INSUFFICIENT INFORMATION flitted across Manders's screen, and his light remained sadly blue.

The door opened and Uncle Bellamy came in, mopping his face with a large handerchief. He stopped and stared. "What on earth is that?" he asked.

"Er . . . Manders made it," said Humbert. "It was meant to be a kite, but I didn't explain it properly."

"It flies," said Manders defensively, pulling the string again.

Humbert thought his uncle wouldn't like the way the bits of paper were swirling around the kitchen but, instead of being cross, Uncle Bellamy held up his arms in the wind and beamed broadly. "Wonderful!" he said. "Just feel that lovely draft!" He bent down to Manders and said, "My dear chap, did you really make this?"

"Yes," said Manders modestly. Then he added, "Not kite. So is what?"

"It's a fan, you twit box," Uncle Bellamy told him. "To keep hot people cool. Just what I needed."

Manders turned cautiously pink. "Good?" he asked.

"Very good," said Uncle Bellamy. "Can I have it upstairs, Hum? Or do you want it for something else?"

"No, you're welcome," said Humbert, and, with some help from Manders, they lugged the contraption upstairs and installed it over Uncle Bellamy's cluttered desk.

"I take it all back," said Uncle Bellamy, collapsing into his chair gratefully as the fan wafted cool air over him. "Manders is marvelous."

"Thank you," said Manders, glowing.

"The only thing is," said Humbert, "all the kite-making stuff has gone into your fan. There's nothing left now except little scraps of brown paper and a lot of string."

"Ah," said Uncle Bellamy, "you have a point." He mopped his face again, thoughtfully. Then he said, "I've got a lot of these big hankies. Actually, they're old sheets. Plenty big enough to make a kite. And you'll need sticks. Now, there used to be a sort of greenhouse out there among the nettles—I expect it's still there. If you send old tin face out to look, he won't get stung. There are lots of garden canes—those thin ones people stick in pots beside geraniums. Ideal for kites."

"Oh, good," said Humbert. "Thank you very much."

"Thank *you*," said Uncle Bellamy, typing happily in his cool breeze.

"Make another kite?" asked Manders as they went back downstairs to the kitchen.

"Yes," said Humbert. "Only this time, I'll stay and help you."

Manders glowed even more. "*Nice!*" he said.

Manders Flies

"I still want to make a kite," said Humbert. "Your first one turned out to be a fan, so we'll have to start again. Let's go and look in the greenhouse. Uncle Bellamy said he thought there were some canes in there."

With Manders following obediently, he went out of the back door—and stopped. "How do you *get* to the greenhouse?" he asked. "There's all these nettles." They stood before him like a forest, shoulder high.

"Walk," said Manders simply, and disappeared into the green forest.

"It's all right for you!" Humbert shouted after him. "I suppose robots don't feel nettle stings!"

The spiky leaves continued to quiver as Manders pushed his way through them, but there was no answer. Humbert ran along the concrete bit outside the kitchen windows to the path beside the high fence between Uncle Bellamy's house and the neighboring one. He hoped the path would lead to the greenhouse and found that it did. The greenhouse faced onto the path, just opposite a gate in the fence.

Manders emerged from the nettles on the far side of the greenhouse just as Humbert arrived at its door. He was hung about with bits of nettle and was feeling his way across the glass with cautious mechanical hands. "Where door?" he asked.

"Round here, you twit!" said Humbert, and Manders plodded toward him. Together, they went into the greenhouse.

"Goodness!" said Humbert. "It's full of cucumbers!" He gazed up in surprise. Tendrils and yellow flowers and big floppy leaves covered the glass, carefully trained up a network of crisscrossing wires. And long green cucumbers hung everywhere.

CUCUMBERS said Manders's screen. WHAT WHAT WHAT WHAT. . . .

"These long green things," Humbert explained, pointing. "You eat them."

"Kind of food," said Manders, satisfied. "Thank you."

"How funny, though," Humbert went on. "If Uncle Bellamy doesn't grow anything in his garden, why has he got this greenhouse full of cucumbers? He never eats them with his sardines." He frowned at Manders, puzzled, but there was nothing on the robot's screen except the words INSUFFICIENT INFORMATION, followed by the question FUNNY? "Oh, don't start whatting about that," said Humbert impatiently. "You either know what's funny or you don't."

A voice from behind him said, "You're right there, boy. And I don't. Not when it comes to my cucumbers."

Humbert jumped. There, in the doorway, stood a large, sagging man. His face sagged and his arms sagged and his clothes sagged, and he looked at Humbert disapprovingly and said, "What are you doing in here?"

"I'm sorry," said Humbert, confused. "I thought this was Uncle Bellamy's greenhouse."

"It is," said the man. "Shocking wicked waste."

Humbert suddenly knew how Manders felt when his screen started whatting. He felt like whatting himself as he gazed at the man in perplexity.

"He doesn't use it," the man explained, "any more than he uses his garden. The people who lived here before him grew a few chrysanthemums in it, but not your uncle. Mice and cobwebs. So I thought I might as well borrow it."

"Yes," agreed Humbert. "I suppose so. Do you live next door?"

"I do," said the man. "Name's Ernie Marvell. I met your mother when she brought you here. She was explaining about that there thing." He nodded at Manders, who nodded politely back.

"He's called Manders," said Humbert. "We came in here to look for some canes to make a kite. Uncle Bellamy said he thought there used to be some."

"Ah," said Ernie. "Matter of fact, Mavis has those. For her geraniums."

"Who's Mavis?" asked Humbert.

"My wife," said Ernie. "She likes things nice, does Mavis. Cucumber sandwiches, she said. Very nice, they are. That's why I wanted to grow some cucumbers, so she can have her sandwiches on the patio, when she comes out of the swimming pool. Like an English stately home."

"Swimming pool?" said Humbert, interested. He liked swimming. "Is there one near here?"

"There's one just the other side of that fence," said Ernie with a jerk of the thumb. "My whole garden's a swimming pool, except for the patio and the pergola and the barbecue. Last year she had everything Spanish, you see. That's why there's no space for growing cucumbers."

"Yes," said Humbert. "There wouldn't be. But what about my kite?"

Ernie sighed. "I'll see what I can find," he said. He fished about under the bench in the greenhouse and produced some bamboo sticks of varying lengths. "These'll do," he said, "I should think."

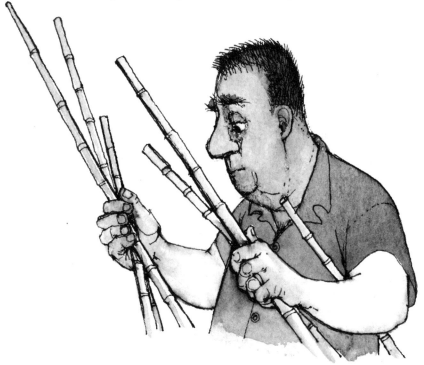

"They're a bit thick," said Humbert.

Manders said suddenly, "Thickness of sticks relative to size of kite."

Humbert stared at him blankly and said, "What do you mean?"

"It's quite right," said Ernie, surprised. "It means the sticks are only too thick if you want to make a small kite. If you make a big one, they'll be fine."

"Will they?" asked Humbert doubtfully.

" 'Course they will," said Ernie. "Takes a practical man like me to understand that sort of thing. Here," he added, thrusting a large ball of hairy string into Humbert's hands, "have some garden twine. You'll need it to tie your crosspieces together. Bring back what you don't use."

"Thank you," said Humbert. "We will."

A voice from the other side of the fence shouted, "Ernest! Have you blown up the raft?"

"That's Mavis," said Ernie, looking alarmed. "It's pool time. I'd better go." He turned back at the doorway and added, "Shut the greenhouse door behind you." And he disappeared through the gate in the fence.

Humbert and Manders took the bamboo sticks and the ball of garden twine and shut the door behind them. Then they went back to the kitchen and set about making a kite.

They had nothing to cut the bamboo sticks with, but they found that the different sizes were more or less right for a long center bit and a shorter crosspiece, with a framework of four more sticks around the outside. They covered it with the old sheet Uncle Bellamy had given them, tying it at the corners securely. Then they made a tail out of more twine and a lot of newspapers.

"Is it right?" asked Manders, inspecting what they had made.

"It's marvelous!" said Humbert. "It's the biggest kite I've ever seen!"

"Good?" asked Manders.

"Very good!" Humbert assured him, and Manders glowed with a satisfied pink light.

They set out for the hill, carrying the huge kite and the rest of the ball of twine. As they walked along the path beside Ernie's garden, Humbert said, "I wonder what the swimming pool is like. I do wish I could see."

"Lift up?" asked Manders helpfully.

"Oh, Manders, could you?" said Humbert.

"Yes," said Manders, propping the kite against the nettles. He grasped Humbert carefully around his middle and, by extending his telescopic arms, raised him up until he could see over the fence.

"That's enough!" said Humbert. Ernie had not exaggerated. The pool did occupy the whole garden except for the concrete bit near the house, where there was a kind of open roof made of timber framework, with creeping plants growing up it, and a lot of potted geraniums and curly white metal furniture with flowered seats. In the pool, floating on a raft, lay a woman in sunglasses with a peacock feather in her hair. She turned her head slightly and saw Humbert.

"Ernest!" she called in a refined voice. "There is a very tall interloper looking over the fence."

"Down!" Humbert said to Manders in a panic. He had wanted only to see the swimming pool. He and Manders picked up the kite and hurried on up the path. Behind them, the gate in the fence opened and Ernie looked out. He stared up and down the path, then went back in. "You can't see a thing through those glasses," they heard him say to Mavis. "I expect it was Bellamy's cat."

Mavis sounded as if she disagreed.

At last Humbert and Manders reached the top of the hill with the enormous kite. Puffing slightly, Humbert said, "Right. Now I'll show you how to fly a kite."

"Thank you," said Manders.

"First," said Humbert, "we tie the string to the middle of the crosspieces. There. Now, you hold the kite, Manders, and don't let go until I tell you. I'm going to walk backward, playing out the string, and when we get a good gust of wind, the kite will go up. We hope."

Walking backward with the ball of garden twine,

Humbert shouted, "Hold it up as high as you can, Manders!"

Manders obediently extended his arms and legs so that the kite was a long way up. The wind caught it with a sudden gust and swept it—and Manders—up into the air.

"Right?" Humbert heard him ask.

Humbert did not get a chance to answer. The kite's string went tight in his hands as it took up all the slack, nearly jerking him off his feet. And in the next instant, the garden twine broke, and the huge kite, with Manders still obediently hanging on to it, went sailing away through the clouds.

Humbert set off after it. Clutching the useless ball of

twine and still holding the end of the broken string, lurching and tripping over things because he could not watch where he was going and still keep an eye on the kite, he ran along the hillside and down a long dirt road. He climbed over a gate, fell into a rut, picked himself up, and ran on, through a farmyard, across a field, over a stile, through a wood where he almost lost sight of the kite altogether, down a path—and suddenly he found that he was almost in Ernie's garden. The kite was dropping sharply because its tail had been catching in the tops of the tall trees in the wood, and Manders was still holding on as he had been told.

"Is this how fly kite?" his distant voice was asking. "Request information."

In the next instant, Manders's dangling feet collided with the chimney of Ernie's house. The kite dived downward and Manders landed with a crash on the open timber framework where the climbing plants grew. His arms and legs thrashed wildly and the kite collapsed on top of him.

"Ernie!" Humbert heard Mavis shriek from her raft in the swimming pool. "There's a helicopter crashed on the pergola!" This time, she did not sound very refined.

Humbert ran on down the path—and almost collided with Ernie, coming out of the greenhouse with a cucumber. He had obviously not heard anything.

"Time for her sandwiches," Ernie said. He took the ball of twine from Humbert and added, "Kite okay, is it?"

Humbert was too out of breath to speak.

"Helicopter!" Mavis was screaming. "Ernie—get a ladder! Ring for the air force! Shoo it off!"

Ernie stared. "What the—" he began.

"I'm very sorry," Humbert gasped. "The string broke."

He watched helplessly while Ernie rushed to get a ladder and climbed up to the pergola, where Manders and the kite were still stuck. Mavis continued to shriek. Manders, Humbert could see, was whatting anxiously, his light flashing bright blue.

"Manders, pull your arms and legs in!" shouted Humbert, seeing that Ernie was having difficulty in disentangling the kite from the robot's hands and feet. "And *let go*!" Manders obeyed at once—and the kite, suddenly free from its obstructions, caught the wind and lifted clear of the roof. But its tail had somehow become knotted around Ernie's ankle.

For a few seconds, Ernie gave a good impression of a climbing plant as he struggled to cling to the pergola. Then the huge kite tugged him free and hauled him through the air after it. But Ernie was heavier than Manders had been, and Humbert watched in horror as the kite and its helpless passenger nose-dived like a pair of diving ducks on to Mavis and the floating raft.

38

Humbert was aghast. The water in the swimming pool had turned into a thrashing mass of arms, legs, string, sheeting, bamboo sticks, and newspaper, with the raft leaping about like a drunken porpoise. He didn't know what to do. Then he saw that Manders was climbing steadily down the ladder from the pergola.

"Please help," said Manders politely to Humbert as he arrived at ground level. "Extend ladder, place across water."

"Oh, yes," said Humbert. "I see."

Quickly, he and Manders got the ladder down from where it leaned against the pergola, and laid it across the swimming pool, its ends resting securely on either side. Ernie reached up from the water and grabbed it, and with the other hand he peeled the kite off Mavis, who was now bubbling rather than shrieking. Manders extended an arm and helped her to the edge, where she clambered out and sat gasping on the patio. Her peacock feather was very bedraggled. Ernie, still in the pool, worked his way hand over hand along the ladder until he reached the steps.

"Ugh," he said as he climbed out with water pouring

from his trousers. "Mavis, we really *must* learn to swim."

"I could teach you," offered Humbert.

Mavis ignored him. She stared at Manders and said, "That thing *isn't* a helicopter, is it?"

"No, madam," said Manders, and handed her a towel he had found hanging over the back of one of the chairs. "I am a Type One Housemaster, at your service."

"Fancy!" said Mavis. She looked at Manders with new interest as she dried herself, then remarked to her husband, "It's got quite nice manners, whatever it is. Do you think we could have one, Ernest? It could serve cocktails on the terrace."

"No, we *couldn't*," said Ernie, dripping. "Bad enough having one next door, doing all the odd jobs I used to do. What would happen to me if we had a thing like that in the house? What would I do all day?"

"I'd find you something," said Mavis, patting her hair. "I always do. Couldn't we get *wicker* furniture for the terrace? This patio set is terribly un-English."

Manders suddenly made a loud buzzing noise. "Food-time," he announced, and started toward the gate.

"Good grief," said Ernie. "Does it eat?"

"No," said Humbert, "he just plugs in every night to charge up his batteries. Manders, do wait a minute. We'll have to get the kite out of the swimming pool."

The words OVERRIDE FOODTIME ran across Manders's screen, and he turned obligingly back, extending a long arm in preparation for fishing.

"*I'll* get the kite out," said Ernie crossly. "You can tell that talking crane of yours to mind its own business."

41

Manders retracted his arm and turned rather blue, and Ernie crawled out across the ladder and leaned down to try and grab the kite. Being thoroughly waterlogged, it had sunk below the surface and he could not reach it.

"Drat," said Ernie.

At that moment, Uncle Bellamy appeared at the gate in the fence. "Hello," he said cheerfully. "Been playing at air-sea rescue? Looks like fun."

"I am not playing at anything," said Ernie crossly. "I am trying to get this blooming kite out of my swimming pool."

"Oh, that's easy," said Uncle Bellamy. "Manders'll do that for you."

"No, he *won't*," said Ernie. "The day I need a tin-faced monster to get things out of my swimming pool, I might as well drop dead."

Manders flashed pink then blue then pink again in a confused sort of way and Uncle Bellamy said amiably, "Suit yourself, Ern. What I came to say is, there's a buzzer making an awful noise in the kitchen. Is it something to do with you, Manders?"

"Yes," said Manders worriedly. "Oven timer, shepherd's pie. Override foodtime." He moved irresolutely to the gate, then back again.

"Let's go and eat, then," said Uncle Bellamy, and Manders's light glowed pink as he led the way back to the house.

Ernie, perched wetly on his ladder, glared after them. "Microchips with everything," he said, but they all pretended they hadn't heard.

Manders had made trifle as well as shepherd's pie, and they were both delicious.

"Mmm," said Uncle Bellamy when they had finished. "Nice change from sardines."

"Goblin doesn't think so," said Humbert, glancing down at the cat. "He's waiting under the table for the tin."

"Shepherd's pie for cat in kitchen," said Manders.

"That robot makes me feel inferior," said Uncle Bellamy when Manders, with Goblin purring beside him, had gone out to do the washing-up.

"I think he's nice," said Humbert. "I wonder if Ernie has got the kite out of the swimming pool yet?"

"Probably," said Uncle Bellamy. "He's a man who gets things done in the end."

"I hope so," said Humbert, "because I haven't actually managed to fly a kite yet. We need much thicker string. Have you got any?"

Uncle Bellamy shook his head. "I'm not the sort of man who keeps graded thicknesses of string," he said.

"No," agreed Humbert.

He collected Manders from the kitchen and went to see what had happened to the kite. It was lying in a soggy heap on the patio—or terrace—and Mavis, in a flowered dress, was drinking tea.

"Enjoying yourself is all in the mind, dear," she said when she saw Humbert. "Ernie won't be long. He's gone to change his trousers." She leaned forward and added confidentially, "Your kite gave him a lot of bother. He fell in again. So then I said he might as well wade for it. Nothing else worked."

"Oh, dear," said Humbert.

Ernie came out of the house combing his still-wet hair. When he saw Humbert he put the comb away in his pocket and said, "You and your blooming kite."

"I'm sorry," said Humbert. "Manders could have got it out for you."

Ernie ignored the suggestion. "Just don't do it again, that's all," he said severely.

"I'll try not to," Humbert promised. "What we need is some thicker string. The garden twine broke, you see."

"What you need is a smaller kite," said Ernie. "You can't fly a thing the size of a ruddy albatross on a windy day like this. Why did you make it so big?"

"Because you said—" began Humbert, and at the same time Manders said, "Thickness of sticks relative to—"

"Oh, all right, all right," said Ernie, exasperated. "Relative to size of kite. I know. If you were going to make a smaller kite, you'd have needed thinner sticks. And it's all my fault." He glared at Manders, who was

nodding agreement, and said, "Does that thing have to be right all the time?"

"Yes," said Manders apologetically.

"Clever little thing, isn't it?" said Mavis, pouring more hot water into the teapot.

"If it's so blooming clever, then why didn't it make a kite that stayed in the air instead of diving into my swimming pool?" demanded Ernie.

"He doesn't really understand kites," said Humbert. "It's a bit difficult to explain what they are."

"Huh!" said Ernie.

Humbert went across to the wet kite and tried to lift it up. It seemed to weigh about half a ton.

"Help?" asked Manders.

"I don't know that there's any point," said Humbert sadly. "Even if we get it back to the kitchen, we can't make a smaller kite out of these thick sticks."

"Can't you give him some thinner ones, Ernest?" asked Mavis, shivering slightly in the freshening breeze.

"They're holding up your geraniums," said Ernie.

"Then find something else," said Mavis, and shook out a large brown rug to put over her knees. It looked as if it had been borrowed from a horse.

"You'd better come into my workshop," said Ernie, and added with an air of gloomy triumph, "I might have known I'd have to do it in the end. Can't expect a walking adding machine to have any common sense. Not when it comes to something like making a kite."

Humbert and Manders (who was whatting uncertainly) followed him into a garage at the side of the house. It was stacked with all sorts of miscellaneous stuff. And there, on a workbench made from the lower half of a piano, Ernie constructed an extremely professional kite of exactly the right size, using the bamboo canes split in half and their crossings bound with specially strong insulating tape, then covered with some gaily patterned thin cotton stuff left over, Ernie said, from a summer when Mavis had wanted everything to be Japanese. "I never did feel right in a kimono," he confessed. He made the kite a tail from twists of fifteen different kinds of surplus wallpaper, then went to a rack

46

on the wall that held balls of string in graded thicknesses. "This should do you," he said, selecting one.

"Thank you," said Humbert meekly.

"Think nothing of it," said Ernie. "Another time, come straight to me instead of wasting your time with old tin brain there." He gave Manders a nasty look and added, "Now, off you go. I'm a very busy man."

Humbert and Manders set off to the hill with the new kite and the ball of correct-thickness string.

"Another time," Manders remarked, "I will know how to make kite properly."

"Of course you will," Humbert assured him. "And I'm going to show you how to fly one, too. It'll be fun."

FUN said Manders's screen. WHAT WHAT WHAT WHAT. . . .

"I can't explain what fun is," said Humbert. "But we're nearly at the top of the hill, and then you'll find out for yourself."

"Thank you," said Manders. "Will it be nice?"

"Very nice," said Humbert.

And it was.

Manders Solves a Problem

"Manders," said Humbert one morning, "can you swim?"

"No," said Manders, his light flashing blue in alarm. "Water bad for batteries. Short circuits." He trembled slightly at the very thought of it and added, "Please not."

"Oh, definitely not," Humbert assured him. "It's all right, I only wanted to know. I just thought I might ask Ernie if we could go swimming in his pool next door, but I won't if you don't fancy it. What shall we do instead?"

"Clean house," said Manders.

Humbert made a face and said, "Do we have to?" This was supposed to be the summer holidays, he thought.

"House dusty," said Manders firmly, and started rooting in the cupboard for polish and bleach and the various specialized cleaning attachments he had brought with him.

"Sometimes," said Humbert, "I wish you weren't a Housemaster. It would be much more fun if you were a Playmaster or something."

Manders turned blue again and said, "Sorry."

There was a tap at the door and Ernie came in. He gave Manders a suspicious look and said, "What's that thing doing?"

"He's going to clean the house," said Humbert.

"Oh, charming," said Ernie, pulling out a chair and sitting down at the kitchen table. "I came to ask your uncle if he wanted me to clean the windows like I usually do, once a month. I suppose Mr. Sponge Fingers here is going to do it instead."

Manders glanced at him doubtfully and muttered, "Ask for advice," then plodded off upstairs.

"Uncle Bellamy won't like being interrupted," said Humbert. "He never does when he's writing."

"What's he actually do, then?" asked Ernie curiously. "I know he's a writer, but I've never seen any books with his name on."

"He writes 'Walter the Wonder Walker,'" said Humbert, "for a newspaper."

"Go on," said Ernie, impressed. "What, in the *Daily News?*"

"That's right," said Humbert. "And he draws the pictures, too. It's about this little fat man in a pin-striped suit and a bowler hat, only he's got sticky feet and—"

"He walks up the sides of buildings," said Ernie. "Rescues secretaries from burning wastepaper baskets and all that. Well, I never."

Footsteps were heard coming down the stairs. Manders opened the kitchen door and stood back politely to let Uncle Bellamy go through ahead of him, which resulted in Uncle Bellamy's tripping over him and

treading on Goblin's tail. Goblin fled under the table with a yowl and Uncle Bellamy recovered himself and said, "Sorry, cat. Not used to these courtesies." He looked particularly ruffled. "What's all this about windows?" he added.

"Fancy you doing Wonder Walker," said Ernie, beaming. "I never knew."

"Of course you didn't *know*," said Uncle Bellamy irritably. "It's bad enough doing the wretched thing without having to talk about it as well."

"D'you get stuck for ideas, then?" inquired Ernie.

"Constantly," said Uncle Bellamy. "Right now, I've got Walter stuck up at gunpoint by a burglar in a penthouse flat in the Finchley Road, and I don't know how I'm going to get him out of it."

"Shouldn't have put him there in the first place," said Ernie.

"I *know*," said Uncle Bellamy, glaring at him.

Manders said diplomatically, "I make tea."

"That thing does all the jobs now, doesn't it," Ernie grumbled as Manders filled the kettle and switched it on. "Pretty bad outlook for the working man."

Uncle Bellamy said innocently, "Oh, sorry, Ern. Did you want to make the tea?"

"I don't make *tea*," said Ernie. "That's the wife's job. I do everything else."

"Then you're not a tea-Ern," suggested Uncle Bellamy.

Humbert giggled.

"Oh, very funny," snarled Ernie. "Anyone can see *you* write for the papers, clever boots."

"That's why I didn't tell you before," said Uncle Bellamy, and glanced at Humbert with faint reproach as he sat down at the kitchen table.

Humbert wished he had not mentioned the Wonder Walker. Trying to make amends, he said to Ernie, "It's nothing personal about the windows. But Manders gets all worried if he doesn't keep everything clean, and puts his blue light on all the time."

"Blue light!" snorted Ernie. "Might as well be sorry for a police car."

"Tea," announced Manders, arriving at the table with a beautifully arranged tray, including biscuits and lump sugar in a bowl with a little pair of tongs.

"One must keep up with the times, you see," said Uncle Bellamy a little smugly. "Robots are modern. Thank you, Manders."

"Gibbering nut box," muttered Ernie, and helped himself to three lumps.

When Ernie had gone grumbling off, Manders washed up the tea things, then filled a bucket with water. "Windows," he announced, and fitted on his sponge and squeegee attachments.

Humbert trailed after him as Manders attacked the windows. He went at it very fast and energetically, as if to prove that a robot could do the job much more efficiently than Ernie Marvell could. When he had finished the ground-floor windows, he carried his bucket upstairs, and Humbert went, too. But Humbert was beginning to feel very bored with window cleaning. This was no way to spend a summer holiday, he thought. What's more, now that Ernie was cross about the windows, it was probably a bit rash to ask him about the swimming pool. "I don't even know if I brought my swimming things," he said gloomily.

"In drawer," said Manders, opening Humbert's bedroom door and pointing. "Second from bottom."

"Thank you," said Humbert. And, having nothing better to do, he bent down to lug the drawer open.

The furniture in his bedroom was heavy and old-fashioned. Humbert suspected that it had been given to Uncle Bellamy by one of the aunts. The curtains that hung at the open window were of maroon plush, and besides the bed and the chest of drawers, there was a washstand with a marble top, an armchair upholstered in dusty velvet, and a tall swing mirror in a mahogany stand. Manders approached this in a businesslike way, dumped his bucket on the floor beside it and rammed a sponge-handed arm out toward the mirror's top.

"Look out!" shouted Humbert.

It was too late. The mirror tilted sharply away from Manders's attacking sponge, and the bottom of it shot forward and swept him off his feet, hurling him clean through the open window. He described a graceful arc above the nettles and fell, with a sickening crash, through the greenhouse roof.

Humbert tore downstairs. Behind him, he heard Uncle Bellamy's door open, but he didn't stop until he reached the greenhouse.

"Manders!" he gasped. "Are you all right?"

"Never mind about Manders!" roared Ernie, who was festooned with foliage and tendrils and floppy yellow flowers like a visitor to the South Sea Islands. "Just look at my cucumbers! Ruined!"

Behind him, Manders had landed untidily on the bench. His screen was showing a procession of rapid WHATs, but they slowed down when he saw Humbert, and he gathered in his arms and legs and turned with single-minded efficiency to the remaining glass of the greenhouse and began to clean it. "Strange window in your bedroom," he remarked over his shoulder. "Same as kite. Made me fly."

"That wasn't a window, Manders," Humbert told him. "It was a mirror. I expect it was *reflecting* the window."

REFLECTING said Manders's screen. WHAT WHAT WHAT WHAT. . . .

"For heaven's sake!" exploded Ernie. "Get that gibbering thing out of here! There's broken glass all over the place."

Uncle Bellamy appeared at the greenhouse doorway

and stared around with interest. "Goodness," he said. "Isn't it amazing how these weeds grow if you just leave them alone? Last time I came in here there were just a few dandelions, and look at them now! Right up to the roof!"

"Those are *not dandelions*," said Ernie, grinding his teeth. "They're—"

"Ah, yes!" Uncle Bellamy interrupted, remembering. "Of course! Hum said you were growing something in here. Spinach, wasn't it?"

"I *was* growing cucumbers," said Ernie. "Until your infernal machine decided to behave like a kangaroo."

"It's a bit odd, that," Uncle Bellamy admitted. "I'm not sure what came over him." He looked up at the jagged hole in the roof and added, "It's quite a mess, isn't it?"

"That's putting it mildly," said Ernie.

Uncle Bellamy scratched his beard thoughtfully and said, "I don't quite understand what's going on. Isn't this supposed to be *my* greenhouse?"

"Well, yes," said Ernie reluctantly. "But you weren't using it."

"No," Uncle Bellamy agreed. "But perhaps you could have just mentioned that you intended to use it. I mean, I might have wanted to keep something in it. A motor bike or a horse or something."

"No point in telling you," said Ernie. "You'd only have forgotten."

Uncle Bellamy sighed. "Yes," he said. "I suppose I would." He stared around at the remaining plants, at least half of which were perfectly all right, and said, "What on earth are you going to do with all these cucumbers?"

"Make sandwiches for Mavis," said Ernie gloomily. "She keeps me on the go, does Mavis. One bright idea after another, she has. Mind you, she's a wonderful woman. Nothing humdrum about Mavis. She wanted me to fill the swimming pool in, you know, and plant a croquet lawn on it, but I said there'd be problems with the drainage." After a pause, he added, "Thing is, she's getting tired of cucumber in her sandwiches. She wants salmon now. Said could I breed them in the swimming pool."

"And can you?" inquired Uncle Bellamy.

"No," said Ernie. "They need miles of fresh running water, with shallow pools at the top and the sea at the bottom."

"Tricky," said Uncle Bellamy. "Won't she settle for fish paste?"

"That's what I suggested," said Ernie. "Salmon-and-shrimp, I said, never know the difference. But no. Not on its own, she said. Only with freshly cut lettuce. And where can I grow lettuce?" He stared regretfully out of the greenhouse at the thicket of nettles and said, "Of course, there's a lot of good land wasted."

Everyone stared at the nettles except Manders, who went on cleaning the greenhouse windows. He was getting very tangled up with the cucumbers.

"I wish you'd tell that thing to stop it," said Ernie, glaring. "It's getting froth all over the leaves."

"That's enough, Manders, thank you," said Uncle Bellamy. Then, as Manders immediately stopped, he added, "By the way, why did you jump through the roof? It seems a bit eccentric, if you don't mind my saying so."

"Window thing," Manders explained, pointing his sponge-equipped hand at Humbert's bedroom. "Upstairs. Start clean it, top go back, bottom come forward, scoop me up, fly me out, land me here."

"Wonderful!" shouted Uncle Bellamy, delighted. "Just the thing for Walter and the armed burglar! He can duck behind the mirror, pull the top back, catch the gunman behind the knees and catapult him through the window! Brilliant! Manders, you've solved a problem. Thank you."

Manders blushed pink and said, "Glad to be of service."

"Well, I wish he'd solve *my* blooming problem," said

Ernie. "I've got a greenhouse full of broken glass and a discontented wife who's bored with swimming, fed up with cucumbers, and pestering me for lettuce. What am I going to do about that?"

"Manders can pick up all the broken glass, for a start," said Humbert practically. "He's got metal fingers, so he can't cut himself. And perhaps he could put a new pane of glass in the roof. It's only one that's broken, even though it looks like such a mess."

"*I'll* replace the glass, thank you very much," said Ernie. "It'll be a lot easier than trying to teach this clockwork monster how to do it. But then, you can't expect a machine to have any common sense, can you? I mean, it isn't human."

"That's not fair," said Humbert quickly, seeing Manders turn blue at such cutting remarks. "There are lots of things he's really good at." He tried frantically to think of something Ernie wouldn't object to on the grounds that an odd-job man could do it better and said rather lamely, "He can walk through nettles and not get stung."

"Can he now," said Ernie thoughtfully. "You don't suppose he can dig them up as well, do you?"

"Dig up nettles, yes," said Manders, brightening slightly. "Gardening program fully inputted in Housemaster. Where start?"

"You'd think it would know where the nettles were," Ernie said to the cucumbers as if even they had more sense than Manders. "Whopping great jungle of them outside, and the silly thing asks where to start!"

Manders moved purposefully to the door and Ernie said, "Oy! Hang on a minute—the boss might want the garden for something else. Keeping a horse. Or a motor bike."

"Not out there, no," said Uncle Bellamy. "There would be problems of straying and rust."

"What about it, then?" demanded Ernie. "Would you mind if I grew some lettuce in your garden?" He added with cunning, "If I put in an extra row, you could have some as well."

Uncle Bellamy shrugged and said, "Why not? I've no *objection* to gardening—I just don't do it, that's all." Gaining enthusiasm for the idea, he added, "We might even have the odd radish."

"And giant sunflowers," said Ernie eagerly. "And hollyhocks."

Humbert remembered something. "You said Mrs.

Marvell wanted a croquet lawn where the swimming pool is," he said. "Well, you could make one here."

"By heck," said Ernie. "You're right. With lettuce around the edge." He turned to Manders and looked at him. "Listen, nut brains," he said, "can you grow grass?"

"Lawn construction inputted," said Manders happily. "What is nut brains, please?"

"Never mind," said Ernie. He reached forward and patted Manders on the head. "You and I are going to make a great team, sunshine," he told him.

"Sunshine needed, yes," agreed Manders. "And watering, and making noises to keep birds off."

"Right," said Uncle Bellamy. "That seems to have solved Ernie's problem. And mine's solved as well. I'm going back to boot the burglar through the window with the bottom edge of the mirror, thanks to Manders. What are you going to do, Hum? Help these two with gardening?"

"I'd rather not," said Humbert. He looked at Manders, who was already picking up the bits of broken glass, then looked at Ernie, who didn't seem cross anymore. "Actually," he ventured, "I was wondering if I could have a swim in your pool."

Ernie took a measuring tape out of his pocket and ran it over the frame of the broken pane of glass. "Far as I'm concerned, you're welcome," he said. "But I don't know what Mavis will say. She's the boss." He looked at his tape and added, "Forty-nine and a bit."

"I'll ask her," said Humbert.

A little later, wearing his swimming trunks, and with a towel rolled up under his arm, Humbert went through the gate in the fence. The sound of Uncle Bellamy's typewriter came busily from his window, and Manders was hewing his way through the nettles like a demented bulldozer. In the greenhouse, Ernie was whistling an unrecognizable tune as he puttied in a new pane of glass.

"Have you come for a swim, dear?" asked Mavis, glancing up at Humbert from her magazine on the terrace.

"Yes, please," said Humbert, "if that's all right."

"Of course it's all right," said Mavis. "Every nice

country house should have children splashing and shrieking in the pool. Actually," she added, "you don't have to shriek. One must not be a slave to convention."

"Thank you," said Humbert. "I'd be quite glad not to shriek." He parked his towel over the back of a curly white chair.

"What's Ernie doing?" asked Mavis.

"He's very busy," said Humbert, and added a little guiltily, "because of something Manders did."

"Really?" said Mavis, impressed. "Busy at what?"

"He's putting a new window in the greenhouse," said Humbert. "And turning Uncle Bellamy's nettle patch into a croquet lawn, with lettuce around the edge. And giant sunflowers and hollyhocks—and the odd radish."

"Oh, thank goodness," said Mavis. She leaned forward confidentially. "Do you know, dear," she said, "it's been a full-time job for years, keeping Ernie busy. Ever since he left the army. He was in the blowing-up squad, you see—ever such a busy job."

"I expect he misses it," said Humbert politely.

"Oh, he does," agreed Mavis. "There's not much blowing-up about, not in Surrey. So I've had to keep inventing new schemes. Digging out the swimming pool was a good one, and building the patio and the pergola, but I've been a bit short of ideas lately. And I'm *sick* of cucumbers."

Humbert wondered whether to tell her that there were not as many cucumbers now, but Mavis didn't stop. "So if that robot of yours is keeping Ernie occupied," she said, "I'm grateful. It really has solved a problem."

65

"He's solved quite a lot of problems today," said Humbert, and dived in. Everyone seemed happy, he thought. And the pool was beautifully warm. He swam about for a bit, then remembered what Mavis had said about splashing and shrieking, and dutifully splashed. He looked up to see if she approved of it, but saw that Mavis was no longer bothered about splashing or anything else. She had fallen contentedly asleep, with the magazine lying face down on the concrete patio beside her chair.

Humbert turned on his back and floated, looking up at the sky with half-shut eyes because of the bright sun. It was turning out to be a good holiday, he thought—thanks to Manders.

Manders Goes Shopping

At breakfast one morning, Uncle Bellamy said, "I suppose we'd better do some beastly shopping."

"Why is it beastly?" asked Humbert.

"Trailing about," said Uncle Bellamy, "and looking at ugly packets with silly names on. Scrump and Yukkies and things like that."

"You don't have to buy Scrump and Yukkies," Humbert pointed out. "And what are they, anyway?"

"I don't know what they are," said Uncle Bellamy irritably. "I made them up. But it's all that sort of thing."

Manders came in with a rack of toast and said, "Toast."

"Well, I didn't think it was compressed custard," said Uncle Bellamy waspishly.

The light on Manders's head turned faintly blue and he said, "Custard not easy to slice."

"It's all right, Manders," said Humbert. "Uncle Bellamy's cross because he's got to go shopping. It's not your fault."

Manders's blue light reverted to white as he thought about this. Then he said, "Why Bellamy shop? I can shop."

"Can you really?" asked Uncle Bellamy, brightening up.

"Yes," said Manders. "Shopping inputted. Please supply money, typewrite list."

"No problem," said Uncle Bellamy. "I'll do that as soon as I've finished my toast. Very nice toast, by the way."

Manders glowed pink and said, "Thank you," and Humbert said, "Custard would never be as crispy."

Manders ignored this remark and went out to the kitchen.

"I do wish he'd laugh sometimes," said Uncle Bellamy.

"I don't think he knows how," said Humbert.

A few minutes later there was a knock at the front door.

"Probably the postman," said Uncle Bellamy, spreading more marmalade.

Humbert heard Manders open the door. There was a piercing shriek from the doorstep.

"Not the postman," said Uncle Bellamy through a mouthful.

"No," Humbert agreed. "He's used to Manders."

Taking his toast with him, Humbert went into the hall. A woman in a flowered hat was clutching her handbag to her chest in alarm as she stared at Manders with bulging eyes. Manders, unperturbed, was repeating for the third time, "Good morning, can I help you?"

"It's all right," said Humbert to the woman. "He's really very nice."

"Good morning, can I help you?" said Manders again, patiently.

"It's a robot," said the woman faintly.

"Type One Super Housemaster," said Manders with a slight bow. "Good morning, can—"

"All *right*," snapped the woman, recovering. She took a deep breath and added, "Well, I knew *something* must have happened. The front gate has been mended, and all the nettles are being cut down—one can actually make one's way up the path. That's why I called."

Humbert heard Uncle Bellamy mutter from the dining room, "I knew Manders shouldn't have cut those nettles down."

The woman did not appear to have heard this. "To be frank, I wondered whether the house had changed hands," she said. "Daphne Panton-Perkins, by the way. I live at Overview Hall. The *large* house, you know. On the hill."

"My name's Humbert," said Humbert. "And this house hasn't changed hands. It still belongs to Uncle Bellamy."

"Ah," said the woman. She seemed disappointed.

"Good morning, can I help you?" asked Manders for the fifth time.

The woman closed her eyes and said, "I really could not speak to a machine." Then she opened them again and said, "It is worse than those telephone-answering devices. The least people can do is answer their own telephones when one wishes to speak to them. Where is

your uncle?" She peered past Humbert and caught sight of Uncle Bellamy, who was trying to sneak up the stairs. "Ah, there he is! Just a moment!"

Manders said quickly, "Please wait. I will inquire." But it was too late. Mrs. Panton-Perkins was in the hall, and Uncle Bellamy had stopped in horror halfway up the stairs.

"I am having a Coffee Morning tomorrow," the woman announced. "In aid of the Tidy Common Fund. All those gorse bushes and silver birch trees—an absolute disgrace. We want to have nice short grass instead and a paved area for supervised ball games."

"Good grief," said Uncle Bellamy.

"So we are charging two pounds a head to attend our Coffee Morning," Mrs. Panton-Perkins went on, "and everyone is to bring cakes or savories. May I count on you?"

"I wouldn't," said Uncle Bellamy. "I'm totally unreliable. And besides, I like the Common the way it is."

Mrs. Panton-Perkins pursed her lips.

"Thank you for calling," said Manders politely, holding the door open. "Good-bye."

Humbert took a bite of the toast he was still holding and tried not to giggle. And Mrs. Panton-Perkins swept out.

Sometime later, Uncle Bellamy appeared in the kitchen. "List," he said, waving a sheet of paper. "Manders, why did you let that frightful woman in? Who was she, anyway?"

"Panting Perkins," said Manders, taking the list. "Not let in. She pushed."

"Panton," Humbert corrected, grinning.

Manders took no notice. He was looking at the list. "What fly-puff?" he asked.

"Stuff to puff at flies," Uncle Bellamy explained, "when there get to be too many of them."

"What fly-pies?" asked Manders, still looking at the list.

"Fly-pies are those flat cake things with currants in the middle," said Uncle Bellamy. "Honestly, Manders, you seem to be a bit dim about this. Are you sure you're all right, shopping on your own?"

"Fully inputted," said Manders confidently.

Uncle Bellamy sighed and said, "You'd better go with him, Hum, just in case."

"I was going to, anyway," said Humbert. "I think it'll be fun."

"Sooner you than me," said Uncle Bellamy. "Oh— you'll need some money. Here—get anything else you think we need." He thrust a large note into Humbert's hand and went back upstairs.

Humbert took the list from Manders and inspected it. "Two dozen tins sardines," he read out, "bread, butter, fly-puff, fly-pies. It seems a bit short."

"Not enough," Manders agreed. "When go shop?"

"Go shop now," said Humbert, lapsing into Manderspeak.

"How go shop?" asked Manders.

"Bus," said Humbert.

The bus conductor stared dubiously at Manders and said, "What d'you call this? Never seen one of them before."

"It's a Type One Super Housemaster," said Humbert. "Two to the supermarket, please. Halves."

"That thing is not a half," said the conductor.

"Half?" enquired Manders, and his screen began a procession of WHATs.

"A half-price ticket," Humbert explained, "for children under fourteen."

"And that contraption is not a child," said the conductor.

"Not fourteen," said Manders politely. "Manufactured this year, age now five months."

"I don't care," said the conductor. "Children are people who are growing up, and that thing is as grown-up now as it's ever going to be. So it isn't a half."

"But he isn't a grown-up," argued Humbert. "He can't be. He isn't even a person."

"Then he's a parcel," said the conductor, "and you'd better put him in the parcel space by the door."

"Can't I have my parcel beside me on the seat?" asked Humbert. "There's plenty of room, and that man over there has got his briefcase beside him."

"You know where you are with a briefcase," said the conductor. "It hasn't got arms and legs."

"But if a briefcase did have arms and legs, could it be on the seat beside him?" persisted Humbert.

"Big shop," said Manders suddenly, looking out of the window and pointing.

"The supermarket!" said Humbert. "This is where we get off. Can I have two halves, please?" He offered the conductor Uncle Bellamy's large note.

The conductor looked at it and sighed. "Just get off this bus," he said. "And don't come back—not with that walking parcel or whatever it is."

Humbert was still arguing as they got off, but Manders waved happily as the bus drove away and said, "Good-bye, thank you." The conductor did not wave back.

"I don't know how you manage to be so cheerful all the time," Humbert said to Manders as they walked into the supermarket. "That man was silly."

"Silly?" asked Manders. WHAT WHAT WHAT. . . .

"Oh, never mind," said Humbert, and pulled a cart out of the stack where they all stood with their noses into each other. He couldn't start explaining silliness with all this music playing, and with Uncle Bellamy's list to add to.

"I don't know what we ought to get," he said.

"Basic household supplies inputted," said Manders. "Shall I get?"

"Yes," said Humbert. "I think you'd better."

Manders plodded along the shelves, scanning them carefully. "Instabubble," he read. "Mixabun, Pufficrackles, Addacherry-Clevvabake, Drinkafome, Fizzagazzy, Big Time Bite. Not food," he said firmly, and steered Humbert toward the shelf labeled Flour. But there, too, he stared at the packets in confusion.

"Earth Fodder, Whole Grits, Momma's Glory," Humbert read out, feeling a bit puzzled himself. "Feather Fingers, Bite-As-Air. This one says Flour—oh no, it doesn't. Flour Substitute for Slimmers. What about Soilfood Husk?"

"No," said Manders. "Where flour?"

"I think they're all flour," said Humbert. "Of sorts. Let's get the one with the picture of a cake on it."

"Cake making inputted," announced Manders as they

selected a packet of Mummy's Little Helper.

"Oh, good," said Humbert. "You could make something for tea, perhaps. Oh, had we better buy some tea?"

People were looking strangely at Manders. An old lady said, "What will they think of next?" and a girl who was stacking the shelves sniffed and said to her friend who was chewing gum and watching her, "I didn't even have a bike when I was a kid, and now they've got robots to play with. All right for some."

Humbert wanted to explain, but Manders was whatting anxiously over the Orange Pekoe and the Cheepcup, and he thought he had better go and help.

They settled for Nopot Nisabags and agreed that the best way of going about the rest of the shopping was for Manders to tell Humbert what to get, then for Humbert to find it on the shelf, because he understood what the names meant.

Gradually the cart filled up with goods. There were

two dozen tins of Hercules sardines (even Humbert didn't understand that one), a pound of Moo butter, a pack of Silvasand sugar and a large bag of O-Shun salt, a dozen Henjoy eggs, and a jar of salad dressing called Yelloyoke. Manders glowed pink at the sight of the ordinary bread without wrappers on it and happily put two loaves into brown paper bags. He was even happier when they came to the produce section and stopped asking for Humbert's help altogether as he selected and weighed and bagged the things he wanted.

Suddenly Humbert heard a voice he recognized. "I would like them *sent*," it was saying. "A very large jar of the cheapest possible coffee and a packet of paper napkins. The guests will bring their own food. What? Of *course* you deliver. You have great big trucks. I've seen them. You can't expect me to burden myself with all this."

Cautiously, Humbert looked around a pyramid of canned dog food called Barker's Bite and saw Mrs. Panton-Perkins arguing with a boy in overalls and a straw hat.

"The trucks deliver to us, Madam," the boy was saying. "You're supposed to take your shopping home in your car."

"Groceries in my *car*?" said Mrs. Panton-Perkins. "What on earth would the chauffeur say? I only came here because I have heard that you are cheaper than Fossett and Gladstone's—but at least they deliver." She glared around, and spotted Humbert. "Ah!" she said, pouncing on him. "The boy I saw this morning. You

will do nicely. You have one of those unpleasant little carts somewhere, haven't you?"

"Manders is putting vegetables in it," said Humbert.

"Then you can add these," said Mrs. Panton-Perkins, and pushed the large jar of coffee and the packet of paper napkins into Humbert's arms. "Oh, and since I don't have to carry them myself, I will have a carton of green olives and some cocktail sticks. There you are. Take them home with you, and I will send a person for them later on today. You can have your food contribution ready as well." She tucked a five-pound note between the coffee jar and the napkins and added, "I shall want the change, mind." Then she stalked off, leaving Humbert openmouthed.

Manders arrived with the cart, which was now very full of fruit and vegetables, together with the fly-puff and fly-pies that Humbert had found. "Why coffee?" he asked. "And what for paper stuff and little sticks? Bellamy not drink coffee. You not drink coffee." His screen was adding up the prices of the things in Humbert's arms, which came to four pounds, ninety-nine pence. "Lot of money," he said.

"I've been silly," Humbert admitted. "I should have told her I wasn't going to carry her things, but she sort of took me by surprise."

"Who?"

"Panting Perkins," said Humbert.

Manders glowed briefly pink and said, "Understand silly now. Yes, you silly."

"Thanks a lot," said Humbert gloomily, and stuffed the extra things into the cart on top of everything else.

"Finished now," said Manders. They pushed the laden cart to the checkout and Humbert could hear him muttering, "Silly man on bus. Silly Humbert. Panting Perkins not silly. Panting Perkins not nice."

The conductor on the homeward bus said, "Two halves. Robots is like dogs." And that was that.

Uncle Bellamy was waiting for them in the kitchen. "There you are!" he said. "Good Lord, what a load!" Then he looked anxious. "You haven't gone and fallen for the Scrump and Yukkies, have you?" he asked.

"No," said Humbert. "We went to a lot of trouble to avoid them."

"I ought to have come with you," said Uncle Bellamy, shaking his head. "I feel rather bad about it. What if you got lost or something?"

"Don't be silly," said Humbert.

"Silly," Manders echoed, recognizing his favorite new word. But his voice sounded faint and the word RECHARGE was flashing on his screen.

"What's the matter with him?" asked Uncle Bellamy.

"I think he's tired," said Humbert, who was feeling quite droopy himself. "Shopping takes rather a lot of energy."

"I tell you what," said Uncle Bellamy as Manders sat down beside the fridge and plugged himself into the wall socket, "you go and amuse yourself for a bit while Manders charges himself up. I'll put the shopping away. It's the least I can do, after you two have gone and got it. And anyway, I know where things go."

"Great," said Humbert, who had seen quite enough shopping for one morning. "I think I'll go and have a swim."

Floating in Ernie's pool, it occurred to Humbert that he had not told his uncle about his meeting with Mrs.

Panton-Perkins. He ought to have explained about the coffee and the paper napkins. Not to mention the olives and the cocktail sticks. Never mind, he thought. He would tell him at lunchtime. He hoped it wouldn't be long. He was getting very hungry.

When Humbert went back to the house, Manders had finished charging himself up and was bustling around the kitchen. "Toad in hole," he announced, whisking open the oven door proudly.

"Lovely," said Humbert. "I'll go and tell Uncle Bellamy."

The toad-in-the-hole was excellent, but the gravy was decidedly strange. "If I didn't know better," said Uncle Bellamy, "I'd say this gravy had coffee in it. Manders, have you run amok in the kitchen?"

"Mock?" inquired Manders. WHAT WHAT WHAT WHAT. . . .

"Amok," said Uncle Bellamy. "Mixed things up. Gone silly."

"Type One Super Housemaster not silly," said Manders with dignity. "This afternoon, make cake." And he left the room, managing to convey that his feelings had been deeply hurt.

Humbert spent an enjoyable afternoon damming the stream until an indignant woman appeared to say that her dahlias were floating down the path. At that point he arranged a controlled overflow system and went home for tea.

The table in the dining room was spread with plate upon plate of buns, scones, and cookies, and Manders stood proudly beside it. "Cake," he announced.

"Good heavens, Manders, I thought you meant one jam sandwich or something," said Uncle Bellamy, staring at the feast. "This is—well—amazing."

"Actually," he confided to Humbert in a whisper when Manders had gone, "I'm not too keen on this sort of thing. Give me a sardine sandwich any day."

"We can always give what's left over to Mrs. Panton-Perkins for her Coffee Morning," Humbert whispered back. "Oh, I didn't tell you. We met her in the supermarket this morning."

Uncle Bellamy was outraged when he heard Humbert's story. "Cheek!" he said. "I wondered why you bought coffee. I mean, we never use it. I tipped it into one of those containers your mother brought. It was half-full already."

Humbert remembered that his mother had spent a long time in the kitchen, explaining to Manders exactly what everything was, and wondered why she had provided coffee. She must have known that her brother didn't drink it. Meanwhile, Uncle Bellamy had picked up an iced bun and bitten into it. His face contorted in horror. "Aaargh!" he said, and returned the mouthful to his hand. "Salt! What on earth has Manders done?"

Cautiously, Humbert took a nibble at another bun, and then at a sample from every plate, and found that everything was so salty as to bring tears to the eyes. "He's got it mixed up," he said, taking a hasty gulp of tea. "Used salt instead of something else."

Uncle Bellamy looked guilty. "Some of those containers might have had labels on them," he said. "New ones your mother put on. But I don't take any notice of that sort of thing. I mean, I know what's what."

"But Manders doesn't," Humbert pointed out. "He has to go by the labels because he can't taste things."

"Design fault," said Uncle Bellamy. He looked at the array of salty cakes and smiled. "I think," he said, "it's time for a sardine sandwich."

"And a fly-pie," said Humbert. "I'll go and get them."

Sneaking into the kitchen a little furtively, Humbert was relieved to see that Manders was out in the garden, hanging up a freshly washed dishcloth. Dipping a finger into the contents of various containers, Humbert soon discovered what had happened.

"You put the salt in a container marked Sugar and the sugar in the Salt one," he reported as he returned to the dining room with the sardines and the fly-pies. "No wonder poor old Manders got it wrong."

"Oh, dear," said Uncle Bellamy. "I'm used to living alone, you see. Don't have to worry about things like that. Can you sort it out?"

"I already did," said Humbert. "The labels are on the lids, so I just switched them over. If we can get rid of this lot, Manders need never know."

"He *is* a robot," Uncle Bellamy reminded him. "I don't think we're going to find him sobbing in the pantry because we didn't eat his cakes."

"No," admitted Humbert, "but all the same . . ."

At this moment Manders appeared outside the French windows with a girl in jeans and said, "This is Lulu. Person from Panting Perkins. For coffee and things."

"Ah," said Uncle Bellamy, jumping to his feet. "I'd better get them. Don't want any mistakes." And he disappeared into the kitchen.

The girl patted Manders on the head and said to Humbert, "He's a hoot, isn't he! Good name he's got for Mrs. P.P. She says she wants something for her Coffee Morning, by the way. Cakes and things. And not to forget the change, she said."

"It's only a penny," said Humbert, fishing in his pocket.

"I know," said Lulu. "That's what she said it would be. She's a mean old bat."

Humbert handed over a penny and suddenly realized that there was a ready-made way to get rid of the salty cakes. "She can have all these," he said, indicating the laden table with a sweep of his hand. Then he turned to Manders and said, "You don't mind, Manders, do you?"

"Mind not inputted," said Manders.

"It's more than she deserves," said Lulu, looking at the table.

"No, it isn't," said Humbert. He almost told Lulu what was the matter with the cakes, but it would have meant telling Manders, too, and, despite what Manders had said about minding, Humbert had a feeling that he would turn his blue light on. It was such a pity, he thought again, that Manders didn't know how to laugh.

Humbert rushed into the kitchen to tell Uncle Bellamy about his idea and found him turning a large plastic container upside down and back again to mix the contents. "Coffee," he explained. "Don't know how long the older stuff has been there, but it'll be all right if it's well mixed in." Humbert told him about the plan for the cakes, and Uncle Bellamy said, "Brilliant."

They came back from the kitchen with Mrs. Panton-Perkins's paper napkins, cocktail sticks, and olives, and with the coffee. They also brought several shopping bags.

"Well, I think it's very nice of you," said Lulu as they put all the scones and buns and cookies into the bags.

"It's not really," said Uncle Bellamy. He looked a little troubled and added, "I hope she won't be cross with you. Come round here if she is."

"She's always cross with me," said Lulu cheerfully as she gathered up the bags. "I don't take any notice. Won't stay long, I expect. Bye-bye." And she went out through the French windows.

"Now," said Uncle Bellamy, sitting down at the table again, "perhaps we can get on with our sardine sandwiches."

Manders came back from seeing Lulu to the gate and said, "Why give away gravy stuff?"

Humbert and Uncle Bellamy looked at each other. "Oh, no," said Humbert. "You didn't put the coffee in with the gravy stuff, did you?"

Uncle Bellamy thumped himself on the forehead with a clenched fist and said, "So that's what the brown stuff was! Well, how was I to know? I thought your mother had absentmindedly given us some coffee." Then he grinned and said, "No wonder the gravy tasted funny."

"Not as funny as Mrs. Panton-Perkins's coffee is going to taste," said Humbert.

"Fetch it back?" asked Manders.

"Er—no," said Uncle Bellamy. "I think we'll leave it where it is."

Manders thought about this for a moment, then said, "You not silly." His pink light flickered brightly and he jiggled up and down.

"What's he doing?" asked Uncle Bellamy.

Humbert looked at Manders, and a smile spread slowly over his face. "I think he's laughing," he said.

Manders Comes Home

"The Common's all right as it is," said Uncle Bellamy. "Nice and wild." He and Humbert were watching Manders help Ernie to sow lettuce seed around the edge of the newly sprouting croquet lawn. "I'd hate to see Mrs. Panton-Perkins turn it into a Games Area. So I'm not sorry we wrecked her Coffee Morning. Well, not very sorry."

"There'll be trouble," said Humbert. Salty cookies and gravy-mix coffee, he thought, were not likely to go unnoticed.

A dilapidated bicycle swerved to a stop outside the house and a girl in jeans got off it. Humbert recognized her as Lulu, who worked for Mrs. Panton-Perkins, and his heart sank.

"I've got the sack," Lulu announced. "Mrs. P.P. is absolutely livid. She said I had to do all the clearing up after the Coffee Morning before I went, but I said if I was getting the sack I'd have it straightaway, thank you."

Ernie finished sowing his lettuce and went back next door, and Manders plodded across to join Humbert and the others, just in time to hear what Lulu said. "Where sack?" he inquired helpfully. "Put in shed?"

"Not that sort of sack, bolt brain," said Uncle Bellamy. "The girl has lost her job. Been dismissed."

Manders glowed blue and said, "Sorry."

"So you should be," said Lulu. "If it hadn't been for your salty cakes and beefy coffee I'd still be there. Not that I'm worried," she added. But Manders had turned a deeper shade of blue. He sat down heavily on the doorstep, and the word WRONG appeared on his screen and stayed there.

"Now you've upset him," said Humbert. "We hadn't told him about the salt." He went and sat beside Manders and said, "It wasn't your fault, honestly. Uncle Bellamy got the containers muddled. You weren't to know."

"Poor thing," said Lulu kindly. "Fancy him taking it to heart like that. You wouldn't think a machine *could*, would you?"

"He's very sensitive," said Humbert.

"Oh, come off it," said Uncle Bellamy. "We all know he's marvelous, but, as Lulu says, he is a machine." He turned to Lulu and added, "I really am sorry about your job. I'm afraid that's our fault."

Lulu gave a cheerful shrug and said, "I expect I'll find something else. I wouldn't have lasted long there anyway. Shall I make you a cup of tea while I'm here?"

Manders said, "Housemaster job make tea."

"Now he's going to sulk," said Uncle Bellamy. "Honestly, Hum, I don't know why your mother thought I needed a machine to organize me. I managed quite well before."

"Ate sardines," said Manders waspishly, and marched into the kitchen after Lulu, who came out rather quickly.

Glancing back, she said, "I worked for a chef once who threw knives."

"Manders wouldn't do anything like that," said Humbert stoutly. "He's very nice."

At that moment Mrs. Panton-Perkins strode up to the gate with her five dogs. She was red-faced and furious. Uncle Bellamy and Lulu both made a dive for the house, but she bellowed, "Stay where you are!"

"Oh, dear," murmured Uncle Bellamy.

"You should be ashamed of yourself!" shouted Mrs. Panton-Perkins.

"Oh, I am, I am," said Uncle Bellamy. "I always have been."

"Not you," said Mrs. Panton-Perkins. "The girl. Lulu, you will come back and clear up after my Coffee Morning. At once."

"You said I'd got the sack," said Lulu. "With no pay."

"So you have," said Mrs. Panton-Perkins. "But you will come and clear up first."

"Blooming well won't," said Lulu.

Manders came out of the house and, seeing a visitor, said, "Good morning, can I help you?"

Mrs. Panton-Perkins looked at him. "Sometimes," she remarked, "I think machines are very much better than people. At least they have manners."

"I know!" said Uncle Bellamy suddenly. "Brilliant idea. *Manders* can clear up after the Coffee Morning. And Lulu can give me a hand. I'm having a terrible morning. I've got pictures all over the floor, because I was looking for a giraffe to see how its tail went. I tried to get Manders to help me tidy them up, but he was useless. Couldn't even sort drawings from photographs."

"I'd like to do that," said Lulu. "It sounds fun. I've never done much except washing-up before."

Mrs. Panton-Perkins snorted. "I do not like *fun*," she said. "People constantly talk about it these days. I hope the machine is not in search of fun. Does it have a leash? Or should I send the chauffeur with the station wagon?"

"Manders isn't a dog," said Humbert crossly. "You just have to talk to him."

"Go with Panting Perkins?" asked Manders doubtfully.

"Yes, please," said Uncle Bellamy. "Now."

"It doesn't pronounce my name very well," said Mrs. Panton-Perkins. "But I expect it will learn. Come along, Thing." And, with Manders plodding behind her, she and the dogs set off up the road.

Humbert watched Manders go, and a cloud seemed to fall across the day, although the sun shone in the sky as brightly as ever.

"You don't mind his doing that, Hum, do you?" said Uncle Bellamy. "It seemed the best way out of a sticky situation. After all, we did wreck the woman's party."

"Not half," said Lulu. "You should have seen people's faces when they tasted that coffee." Then she added, "Where's these pictures, then?"

"In the office," said Uncle Bellamy, and led the way indoors.

Without Manders, it seemed a long day. Humbert went and looked at his dam across the stream, and then he looked at his kite and wondered whether to fly it, but somehow he couldn't be bothered. He would have liked to go and explore the Common, but it wouldn't be much fun on his own. After a while, he decided to have a swim in Ernie's pool, and when he got back, Lulu had made sardines on toast for them all.

"Jolly good cook, isn't she?" said Uncle Bellamy, munching happily.

Humbert wondered if Manders was cooking one of his delicious lunches for Mrs. Panton-Perkins. Surely he should be back by now? When he had finished his sardines, he went out and hung over the gate, eating an apple and looking up the road for Manders. At last he gave up and went for another swim.

"Where's your little friend today?" asked Mavis, who was drinking something out of a tall glass with a cherry in it.

Humbert climbed out of the pool and explained gloomily what had happened.

"Shame," said Mavis. "I do hate people who don't like fun. Come and join me in a Pink Fizzerama. It's my latest way to keep Ernie busy. Fancy drinks with lots of

ice and fancy names. He made a Peppy-poppy Ticklebanger yesterday."

"What's that?" asked Humbert, rubbing his hair with a towel.

"You have to smash up lots of peppermints with a rolling pin," explained Mavis, "then put them in the mixer with egg white and ice cream and green jelly and whiz it up with lemonade. It takes ages. Ever so good for him. I say, do cheer up. You look really mopey."

Humbert managed a halfhearted smile. The Pink Fizzerama was very nice. "They all think Manders is just a machine," he said. "And, I mean, he *is*, but . . ."

He shook his head. It was difficult to explain what Manders was.

"I know what you mean," said Mavis. "He's your mate, isn't he? Never mind. He'll be back soon. Have some more fizz."

But Manders was not back by teatime, and Humbert munched his way through another lot of sardines on toast in deep gloom. Then the telephone rang, and Uncle Bellamy went to answer it. "Oh, good," Humbert heard him say. "Yes. Glad about that." Then, after a long pause, "Well, I don't know. Not mine to sell, you see." There was another long pause, then, "Yes, okay. Bye."

"Mrs. Panton-Perkins," said Humbert as his uncle came back.

"Too right," said Uncle Bellamy. "Panton-Nonstop-Perkins. Can't get a word in edgeways. She wants to buy Manders."

"She *what*?" shrieked Humbert.

"Sit down, sit down," said Uncle Bellamy, flapping at him. "I told her it wasn't up to me."

"But she *can't*," said Humbert, subsiding but still alarmed. "I mean, Manders is *ours*."

"I don't really know whose he is," said Uncle Bellamy, scratching his beard thoughtfully. "Your mother supplied him to look after us while you came for this holiday, so I suppose he belongs to her."

"Or perhaps she just borrowed him," said Humbert, "from that man called Trev." He gazed at his uncle in horror. "You don't suppose he'll have to go *back*, do you?"

"I've no idea," said Uncle Bellamy. "I never know what other people are going to do. I think they're all mad."

"I must find out," Humbert said frantically. "Mum's still away doing her grass talks. Perhaps I could ring my father."

"Do," said Uncle Bellamy.

Humbert dialed his number, and the telephone rang and rang, but nobody answered it. He replaced the receiver and said, "He's not there."

"I expect he's doing something important," said Uncle Bellamy. "He usually is. Try again later."

Humbert tried again several times, but his father was still not in, and at last it was time to go to bed.

"Don't worry," said Uncle Bellamy. "Manders will be quite all right, you know. He's lucky. If he feels a bit down, he has only to plug himself into a power point, and then he's fine again. Wish I could do that."

Humbert said, "Yes, it would be handy, wouldn't it." But he was still worried.

Uncle Bellamy looked at him, then said kindly, "I know he's your friend, Hum, but really, he isn't quite like a person. You mustn't fret about him. He doesn't feel things like you do."

Humbert nodded slowly, but he was not convinced. Uncle Bellamy was very nice, but he didn't understand Manders. None of them did.

The next morning, Lulu was in the kitchen when Humbert and Uncle Bellamy came down. "I've made the tea," she announced, "and they sent the wrong paper,

so I've been down and changed it, and here's your letters. I threw away the advertising ones about slipcovers and encyclopedias. I knew you wouldn't want those."

"Marvelous," said Uncle Bellamy. He turned to Humbert and added, "You see, that's the sort of thing Manders can't do."

"But I don't want Manders to do things like that," Humbert objected. "I mean, I don't *get* letters about slipcovers. I just like him to talk to and do things with. We could have explored the Common if only he'd been here."

"Where is he?" asked Lulu. "Not still with old toffee nose?"

"Yes," said Humbert. "And she wants to keep him." He told Lulu all about it as he helped her take things in for breakfast, and she tutted sympathetically.

"You can see why she likes him," she said. "He does exactly as he's told, and he'll work all day and night so long as he's charged up from time to time, and she doesn't have to feed him or pay him."

"I know," lamented Humbert. "He's just too good. She'll never want to give him back."

Lulu put four slices of toast in the rack and said, "We'll have to think of something."

"Yes," said Humbert and took the toast in to where Uncle Bellamy sat opening his letters untidily all over the table.

After breakfast, Humbert stood by the sink while Lulu did the washing-up, and said, "There's only one way to get him back. I'll just have to go and fetch him."

"Good idea," said Lulu.

"The trouble is," Humbert went on, "he's so conscientious. If Mrs. Horrible says he's to stay, he'll probably feel that he's got to."

"You'll just have to tell him it's wrong for him to be there," said Lulu. "Be firm. But with any luck, you won't see the old horror, anyway, not if you go in through the side door. I'll show you where it is." And she explained in detail, drawing a map in the soapsuds with her finger.

"Lulu!" shouted Uncle Bellamy from his office. "Can you find me a picture of a helicopter somewhere? I've got a letter from a reader here, saying the one I drew last week would have fallen out of the sky."

"Coming!" said Lulu, drying her hands.

"See you later," said Humbert, and went out the back door.

101

He found his way to Overview Hall quite easily and walked up the drive between the rhododendron bushes. Curved flights of steps with stone lions at the top led up to the front entrance, but Humbert skirted carefully around the lawn, following the gravel path that led to the side door. There, he tapped cautiously.

The door was opened by Manders, who wore a stiffly starched white apron and a frilly cap. "Good morning, can I help you," he said, then suddenly glowed pink. "Humbert," he said. "Very nice. Good. Thank you. Please come in."

"Why on earth are you wearing those things?" asked Humbert as he entered the kitchen, which seemed about the size of Waterloo Station.

"Madam says uniform required," said Manders, his pink light fading.

"Who's Madam?" asked Humbert. "Mrs. Panton-Perkins?"

"Panting, yes," said Manders. "Madam." And he gave a slight, respectful bow.

"Manders, you can't stay here," said Humbert. "I've come to take you home."

"Home not allowed," said Manders, whose light was now turning blue. "Madam says this home now. Must do as told."

"That's what I thought," said Humbert gloomily.

At that moment a bell rang from upstairs and Manders said, "Panting wanting something. Must go. Yes, Madam." And, despite Humbert's protests, he hurried out of the room.

Humbert frowned. This was not going to be easy. From above him, he heard a wild scrabbling of claws and a chorus of barking, which got rapidly louder until the door burst open and the five dogs charged in. Manders, clutching their leashes in both hands, tumbled in behind them. "Dogs for walk," he announced. "Madam says."

"Then I'll come, too," said Humbert firmly. "I want to talk to you."

"Nice," said Manders. He opened the door and the dogs rushed out, towing him behind them. "Please shut door," he said over his shoulder. It was amazing, Humbert thought, how he always managed to sound calm. But then, as people kept saying, he *was* a machine.

"Wait for me!" Humbert shouted, but Manders was bouncing across the lawn in the wake of the five dogs and seemed unable to answer.

Humbert rushed after him. "Let them off their leashes," he suggested. "Then you won't have to run so fast."

"Madam said not let go," explained Manders. "In case all run away."

"Then give me a couple of their leashes," said Humbert breathlessly. "Perhaps we can slow them down between us."

"Madam said—" began Manders.

"Oh, blow what Madam said!" Humbert exclaimed, running to keep up. "Listen, Manders, you know what WRONG means, don't you?"

"Yes," said Manders. "Wrong inputted."

"Well, it's wrong, your being here," panted Humbert. "My mother meant you to be with Uncle Bellamy and me, not with Mrs. Panton-Perkins."

"Madam wrong?" inquired Manders, tripping over a dog that stopped suddenly to raise a leg against a statue of a nymph.

"Yes," Humbert insisted as they charged off again. "Madam wrong. You wrong. Everything here wrong."

The light on Manders's head turned pink then blue then pink again in a confused sort of way. "Wrong," he murmured. "Everything wrong."

They galloped around the corner of the potting shed and found themselves at the back of the house. A long ladder leaned up against the wall, and at the top of it a man was painting the window frame of an upstairs room.

"Look out!" Humbert said urgently. "Mind the dogs!"

Manders did not appear to notice. "Everything wrong," he muttered again and careened on behind the dogs that, as Humbert had feared, ran on either side of the ladder. Their leashes brought Manders slap up against the bottom of it. He let go of the dogs and clutched for support at the ladder, which swayed drunkenly, complete with the man who still clung, shouting, to the top of it. Then it keeled sideways and fell to the ground, catapulting the man into a yew bush clipped to the shape of a peacock.

Mrs. Panton-Perkins flung open the French windows and shouted, "Get off my peacock!" And at this precise moment, the pot of paint, which had teetered on the windowsill above her since the painter had so suddenly abandoned it, finally fell off. It landed upside down on her head.

"Jarvis!" she bellowed. "You idiot!"

"Wasn't my fault," Jarvis protested from his peacock. "It was that there nit-brained machine of yours. Knocked me off my ladder."

"Don't just sit there!" screamed Mrs. Panton-Perkins, dripping. "Thing, get a towel! Hurry!"

Manders plodded thoughtfully toward the kitchen, and Humbert, hiding behind a stone urn, wished he could reach him. This, he thought, would be a very good time for both of them to go home, before Mrs. Panton-Perkins recovered.

Unhurriedly, Manders reappeared and held out a single square of paper towel.

"You mindless cretin!" shrieked Mrs. Panton-Perkins.

"Can't you see what a mess I'm in? That's no use—get something to clean me up!"

This time, after an even longer pause, Manders came back with an armful of cleaning materials. Mrs. Panton-Perkins, with her eyes screwed up, was wiping her face with the net curtain that hung at the French windows. Manders selected a tin of scouring powder and sprinkled it over her hair. Jarvis, sitting comfortably on his rather squashed peacock, giggled. Manders followed this up with several squirts of dishwashing liquid and a long spray of aerosol polish, then topped off the whole effect with an immense meringue of upholstery foam from a thoroughly shaken can.

It was some moments before Mrs. Panton-Perkins realized what he had done. Then, dripping foam as well as paint, she gave a loud scream and, with a sweep of the paint-spattered curtain, she knocked him off his feet. He landed in a bed of geraniums, where he lay on his back with his pink light flashing and the word WRONG illuminated unrepentantly on his screen.

Jarvis got down from the peacock and said, "Reckon you'll need some turps."

"Then *get* some, you blithering nincompoop," shouted Mrs. Panton-Perkins between screams, and began hurling a variety of things from the sitting room at Manders. Most of them either missed or bounced off, but a tiger-skin rug landed on top of him and heaved up and down over his kicking legs in a most threatening way. The dogs took one look at it and fled, howling.

"Go away!" Mrs. Panton-Perkins bawled at Manders as Jarvis produced a gallon of turpentine substitute and poured it slowly over her head. "Leave my house, and don't come back! Next time I employ a Thing I shall get a new one, not a shop-soiled, fault-ridden item like you. Jarvis, be *careful*!"

Manders rose to his feet with dignity. "Type One Super Housemaster not shop-soiled," he said. "First-grade quality." And he set off toward the gate, apparently unaware that the tiger-skin rug had somehow attached itself to his head, its nether parts trailing in the gravel behind him. This, combined with the fact that he was still wearing his frilly apron, made him look decidedly strange and, as he emerged on the road, a passing cyclist fell into the ditch at the sight of him.

Humbert, by ducking behind rosebushes and stone urns and statues, managed to get out unobserved and caught up with Manders. "You were marvelous!" he said.

"Not marvelous," said Manders modestly. "Just wrong." He stopped and thought for a moment, his light glowing with effort from behind the tiger's whiskers. Then he said, "With you and Bellamy, wrong not right? Wrong wrong? Right right?"

"Oh, yes," Humbert assured him. "Right right." And, hand in hand, they went home.

"Hello, dear," said Mavis from her patio as she saw Humbert and Manders coming into their garden. "You found your little friend, then. I say, I like that tiger skin. What a good idea. I could have a summer in India, couldn't I, with a mongoose in the bathroom and a three-bladed fan circling slowly under every ceiling. That would keep Ernie busy for ages. I might even buy him a cobra."

Humbert said cautiously that he didn't think a cobra would like it much in Surrey, and Mavis nodded agreement. "Just a few monkeys, then," she said. "And a ruined temple for them to live in. Ernie could build that, too."

Humbert wasn't sure about the monkeys, either, but he didn't want to get dragged into a long conversation. He and Manders went into the kitchen, where Lulu was opening a tin of sardines. She looked up and saw the tiger skin and said, "Oh, crikey, you gave me quite a turn."

Manders ignored this. He marched firmly across to the table, gave the tin of sardines to Goblin, and announced, "I will make lunch."

"Oh, *good*," said Humbert.

113

As he was finishing the last of his spaghetti, Humbert glanced out of the window and saw a Rolls Royce draw up outside.

"That'll be Mrs. You-know-who," said Lulu. "Come for her cat."

"Leave this to me," said Uncle Bellamy, and strode masterfully to the door, with Humbert close behind him.

Mrs. Panton-Perkins, looking very freshly shampooed, glared at Uncle Bellamy and said, "You have stolen my tiger-skin rug. And a housemaid's cap and apron. Frilled."

Uncle Bellamy had no idea what she was talking about, having been shut away in his office when Humbert and Manders came back from Overview Hall. He blinked and said, "Can you in your wildest dreams imagine me as a housemaid? Let alone Tarzan. And tiger skins belong on tigers. The idea of their being anywhere else is quite disgusting. Really, dear lady, I think you are off your head."

Humbert went into the kitchen to fetch the rug and the cap and apron, which Lulu had tied into a neat bundle with a piece of string. When he got back, Mrs. Panton-Perkins was still shouting at Uncle Bellamy, who was wilting perceptibly.

"—and the robot is a heap of rubbish," she declared. "I have rung up the manufacturers and demanded compensation for damage to my person. And to a bush clipped to the shape of a peacock. It now looks like a duck. Very uncooperative people. Positively rude."

"Who did you speak to?" asked Humbert. "Was it a man called Trev?"

"I have no idea," said Mrs. Panton-Perkins. "These people do not deserve to have *names*. He had the cheek to suggest that if the Thing misbehaved, it was *my* fault. Huh!" She snatched the bundle from Humbert and swept off down the path. "The Hall," she commanded the chauffeur as she stepped into the Rolls Royce. "And

do not waste gas by pausing at these stupid zebra crossings. Just hoot."

Speechlessly, Humbert and Uncle Bellamy watched the huge car zoom away up the road. And then the telephone rang.

"Answer that, Hum, would you," said Uncle Bellamy, mopping his brow with one of his enormous handkerchiefs. "I think I'm having a nervous breakdown."

It was a loud, cheerful voice that spoke in Humbert's ear. "Trev here—your dad's friend, know who I mean? What's all this about the Housemaster? Just had a funny phone call. It's all right, isn't it?"

"Oh, yes," said Humbert. "He's fine." And he explained what had happened.

"Yes," said Trev. "It sounded like some nutter. They're pretty reliable, those Type Ones—only I thought I'd just check, because your dad's earmarked that one for when your holiday's over."

"Has he?" said Humbert nervously. "What for?"

Trev laughed. "For himself," he said. "He got into a terrible muddle trying to run the house with your mum away. You know what he's like—brilliant at business, but not a practical man. In fact, he gave up the struggle and came to stay with me and Marjorie."

"So *that's* why I couldn't get him on the phone," said Humbert.

"Right," said Trev. "Your mother sent him a postcard saying her grass talks are a big success. People want her to do a lot more of them. Well, that finished him. Got to have some help, he says. So he wants the Type One Super Housemaster permanently. It's to come home with you at the end of the holidays. Unless your uncle has become attached to it, that is."

118

"Oh, he hasn't, he hasn't," Humbert burbled happily. "He likes Lulu better because she can sort his pictures out and she makes sardines on toast."

"Great," said Trev. "I'll tell your old man it's okay, then. Cheers!" And he hung up.

Humbert rushed into the dining room, where Lulu was assuring Uncle Bellamy that he had been wonderfully brave and calm and deserved a medal. "Manders is coming home!" he said. "For always! Isn't it marvelous!"

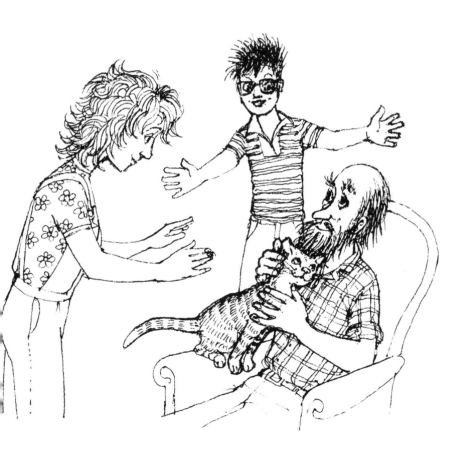

"Oh, smashing," said Lulu. "I'm really glad."

"Not Panting anymore?" inquired Manders.

"Never," Humbert assured him. "You're coming to live with me."

Manders glowed bright pink and jiggled up and down, and the words GOOD GOOD GOOD GOOD GOOD traveled across his screen.

"Well, I'm blowed," said Uncle Bellamy. "Seems you were right, Hum. He does have feelings. Look at him—he's happy."

"Of course he is," said Humbert.

"Actually," said Uncle Bellamy thoughtfully, "although I am a great admirer of the sardine, as you know, it might be a good idea if he gave Lulu a few cooking lessons before you went. That spaghetti was a bit of all right—for a change, you know."

"Be great if you could," Lulu said to Manders.

Manders, still glowing, bowed graciously. "Cooking lessons inputted," he said.

"That's all right, then," said Humbert.

"I must get some work done," said Uncle Bellamy. "I've wasted quite enough time on the demented person with the overblown car. What are you going to do, Hum?"

"I thought I'd like to explore the Common," said Humbert, "if it's nice and wild."

"Go now?" asked Manders.

Humbert smiled. That was the great thing about Manders. He was always ready for anything. "Go now," he said.

And they went.